WOLFIE

Janet Chenery

Illustrated by Marc Simont

A YOUNG YEARLING BOOK

Published by
Dell Publishing
a division of
Bantam Doubleday Dell Publishing Group, Inc.
666 Fifth Avenue
New York, New York 10103

For Ted and Will

ISBN: 0-440-40496-7

Reprinted by arrangements with the author and artist

Printed in the United States of America

July 1991

10 9 8 7 6 5 4 3 2 1

WES

WOLFIE

Harry and George sat

in their secret meeting place.

It was a large doghouse

for Harry's dog.

But Biffy never used it,

so Harry and George did.

5

"How many flies did you catch?"

asked Harry.

"Three," said George.

He pulled a small bottle

out of his pocket.

"Only three?" asked Harry.

"We will need more than that."

George sighed.

"It took me an hour to catch these.

Are you sure he likes flies?"

"Sure," said Harry.

"Don't you remember?

The book said that spiders eat

live flies and other insects."

"Yes," said George. "But the spider

in the picture had a web.

Wolfie hasn't made a web yet."

"He will make a web

when he sees the flies," Harry said.

He picked up a big jar.

Something inside it moved.

"Hello, Wolfie," Harry whispered.

He unscrewed the jar lid carefully.

"Get ready," he told George.

George turned his bottle upside down

over the big jar.

He took off the bottle top

and shook the flies into the jar.

Harry quickly put the lid back on.

"Have a fly, Wolfie," said Harry.

They watched the brown spider

in the jar.

At first it did not move.

Then it made a dash at the fly.

But the fly got away just in time.

Outside the doghouse

someone called, "Harry!"

"Shh! It's Polly," Harry whispered.

"Hide Wolfie!"

Polly was Harry's little sister.

"I want to see the spider," she said.

"No!" said Harry. "Go away! Scram!"

"Wait, Harry," George said.

Then he stuck his head

out of the doghouse.

He said to Polly,

"You can see Wolfie.

But first you have to bring him

a hundred flies.

Live ones."

"Okay," said Polly, and off she ran.

"Why did you tell her that?"

asked Harry.

"Now she'll pester us all the time."

"No, she won't," said George.

"It's very hard to catch flies."

"You don't know Polly,"

Harry grumbled.

They watched Wolfie for a while

to see if he would eat the flies.

"Wolfie looks sad," said George.

"Maybe we need a bigger place

to keep him."

"Let's ask my mother

if she has anything bigger,"

Harry said.

Polly was at the kitchen table.

She had a rubber band

over her first finger.

She pulled the rubber band back

like a slingshot.

A fly walked across the table.

Snap! Polly let the rubber band go.

The fly bounced over on its back.

"Wow!" said George.

Polly picked up the fly

and put it into a jelly jar.

There were four other flies

in the jar.

"They have to be alive," said Harry.

"Wolfie won't eat dead flies."

"They are alive," said Polly.

"They are just stunned."

She shook the jar. The flies buzzed.

Harry gave George a dirty look.

"What did I tell you," he said.

Harry asked his mother,

"Do you have anything bigger

than a jar for Wolfie?"

"Who is Wolfie?" his mother asked.

"He is a big hairy spider,"

said Harry.

"Harry won't let me see him,"

Polly said,

"until I catch a hundred flies."

"A spider!" said Harry's mother.

"Where is it?"

"In Biffy's house," said Polly.

Harry's mother said,

"Why don't you take it to Miss Rose
at the Nature Center?
Biffy and Inky are enough pets
for one family."

"Anybody can have a dog and a cat,"
Harry said.

Polly snapped her rubber band
and stunned another fly.

"Can I go to the Nature Center too?"
Polly asked.

"No!" said Harry.

He and George ran outdoors.

The Nature Center had rocks,
butterflies, other insects, and leaves.
When they got there, George said,
"Miss Rose, do you have something
we can keep Wolfie in?"

"Who is Wolfie?" asked Miss Rose.

"Wolfgang," Harry said.

"He is a wolf spider."

"Really?" Miss Rose asked.

"How do you know?"

"We looked him up in a book,"
George said.

"He's big and brown and hairy,"
said Harry.

"And he runs very fast.
We saw him chase a bug,
and he caught it too."

"What are you feeding him?"
Miss Rose asked.

"Flies," George said.

"But they are very hard to catch."

"What about water?" asked Miss Rose.

"Water?" asked Harry.

"Do spiders drink water?"

"Yes, they need water as much
as they need food," said Miss Rose.

"I don't think he's very hungry,"
George said. "He hasn't made a web
to catch flies."

"He won't spin a web if he is

a wolf spider," said Miss Rose.

"Some spiders spin webs

to trap insects,

but wolf spiders run after them.

They are hunters.

Wolf spiders do not

trap insects in a web."

"Then what should we keep him in?"
asked Harry.

"The best thing would be a big box
with a wire screen over the top,"
Miss Rose said.

She showed them what to do.

Miss Rose picked up a small screen.

"Here," she said. "You can use this.

When you have Wolfie all fixed up,

will you bring him here?

I'd like to see him."

"Okay," Harry said. "Thank you."

When Harry and George got home,

they found an old wooden box.

They put some dirt in it.

They added twigs and leaves

and a little clump of grass.

While Harry held the screen

George dumped Wolfie

into his new home.

Wolfie ran into a corner

and hid under a leaf.

"Let's get him some food,"

said Harry.

"And water," said George.

"How do you give spiders water?"

"I know," said a voice.

It was Polly.

She was sitting on the grass

with Biffy and Inky.

"Go away!" said Harry.

"How *do* you give water to a spider?"

asked George.

"You put drops of water on a leaf,"

Polly said. "Sometimes

Inky drinks dewdrops that way."

30

"Okay, go get water," Harry said.

"Bring some flies too,"

George said.

Polly brought back a jar of flies

and a glass of water.

"I got seven flies," she said.

"Can I watch you feed Wolfie?"

"No," said Harry.

"You have to get a whole hundred."

George and Harry put the flies

into Wolfie's box.

They sprinkled water on the leaves.

Wolfie turned around.

One of his legs touched a wet leaf.

He seemed to be breathing heavily.

He bent his knees.

Then he touched the wet leaf.

"He's drinking the water!"

George said.

Wolfie made a dash at a fly.

"He got him!" Harry shouted.

"Boy, is he fast!"

The next day Harry and George

took Wolfie to Miss Rose.

"You were right," Miss Rose said.

"It is a wolf spider.

Did you notice

how many eyes he has?"

"Eyes?" said George.

"Don't insects have two eyes?"

"A spider is not an insect,"

Miss Rose said.

"What is it then?" Harry asked.

"An *a-rach-nid*," said Miss Rose.

"Most wolf spiders have eight eyes.

Bring him over to my worktable,

and I will show you."

George and Harry took Wolfie's box

to the table.

Miss Rose got a magnifying glass

and held it over the spider.

He looked enormous,

very hairy, and quite cross.

Harry counted.

Wolfie had eight eyes.

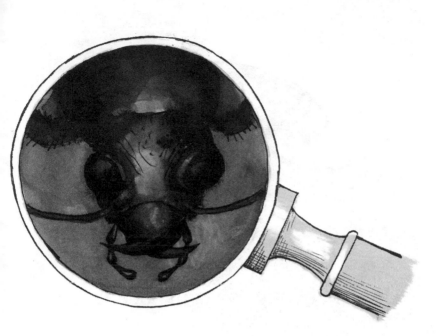

Miss Rose reached into a glass tank

and picked up a shiny black beetle.

It waved its legs.

Miss Rose took the magnifying glass

and held it over the beetle

so Harry and George could see it.

"How many legs does the beetle have?"

she asked.

Harry and George counted.

"Six!" they said together.

"How many does Wolfie have?"

Miss Rose asked.

"Those two things near his head—

are they his legs?" asked George.

"No, those are palps.

Wolfie sometimes uses them

to hold his food."

"Well then, he has eight legs,"

Harry said.

"Right," said Miss Rose.

"Spiders have eight legs.

Insects have six."

"Is that what makes spiders

and insects different?"

asked George.

"Just the number of legs?"

"No," said Miss Rose.

"There are other differences.

Take a good look at Wolfie.

How many parts does his body have?"

"He's got a head," said Harry.

"And a body," George added.

"Now look at the beetle,"

said Miss Rose.

"How many parts does it have?"

The beetle wriggled in her fingers.

"He has a head, but his body

has two parts," said George.

"So he has three parts altogether,"

said Harry.

41

"He has feelers on his head too,"
said George.

"Wolfie doesn't have feelers."

"That's right," Miss Rose said.

"Those don't seem like
very big differences," said Harry.

"How else are they different?"

Miss Rose put the beetle down gently
in his glass box.

"Look again," she said.

She put the wire screen back
over the top.

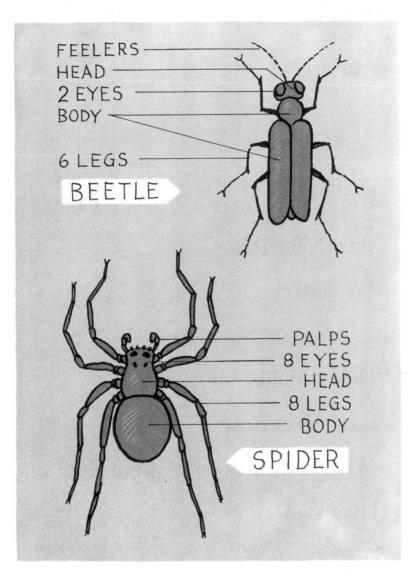

FEELERS
HEAD
2 EYES
BODY
6 LEGS
BEETLE

PALPS
8 EYES
HEAD
8 LEGS
BODY
SPIDER

"Why did we put screens over
Wolfie's box and my beetle's tank?"
asked Miss Rose.

"So they can have air
but can't get out," said George.

"How would they get out?"
asked Miss Rose.

"Why, Wolfie would climb right out,"
Harry said.

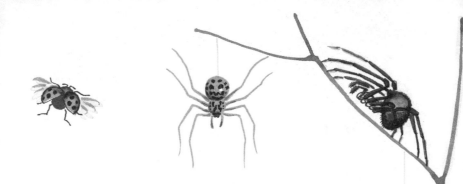

"The beetle would too," George said.

"Or he could fly out—"

"That's it!" cried Harry.

"Wolfie can't fly!

He doesn't have wings."

"Right you are, Harry,"

said Miss Rose.

"Spiders don't have wings,

but many insects do."

Harry and George took Wolfie

back to the doghouse.

Every day they watched him

and fed him the flies

that Polly had caught.

One day she caught seven,

and another day she caught five.

But she did not catch

anywhere near a hundred.

So Polly asked Harry again,

"Can't I see Wolfie now?

I have twenty-seven flies."

"No," said Harry. "One hundred."

"Why?" Polly asked.

"You showed him to Miss Rose.
She didn't catch any flies for him."

"Of course not!" Harry said.

"Miss Rose knows all about spiders!
Besides, she's not a pest like you!"

"I am *not* a pest," cried Polly.

"Yes, you are," Harry said.

"Go away, pest."

Polly did not catch any more flies
for Wolfie that day.

When Polly went to bed,

she was still mad at Harry.

Inky jumped on her bed.

"Harry is mean," she told Inky.

"Who wants to see his old spider

anyway?" she said.

In the middle of the night

Polly woke up.

She thought about Wolfie

and the flies she had to catch

before Harry would let her see him.

Inky woke up and meowed softly.

Polly slipped out of bed

and got her flashlight.

Inky followed her.

They tiptoed out of the room,

down the stairs, and out the back door.

Silently, they crossed the yard
to the doghouse.
Polly shined her flashlight inside.
She crawled in
and held the light
over Wolfie's box.
"Hello, Wolfie," she whispered.

Harry woke up too.

The moon made shadows in his room.

The shadows looked like big animals

with long wavy legs.

Harry remembered

he had not given Wolfie any water.

He got out of bed

and found his flashlight.

He got a glass of water

and crept down the stairs.

The back door squeaked.

Harry hoped his parents

would not wake up.

Polly heard Harry coming.

She turned off her flashlight

and held Inky close to her.

Everything looked very different

to Harry in the moonlight.

The house seemed large,

and the trees looked like giants.

The doghouse was very dark
and silent.

Harry got down on his knees
to crawl inside.

He pointed his flashlight
at the entrance.

Two yellow eyes stared at him.

Harry remembered how Wolfie looked
under the magnifying glass.

He almost stopped breathing.

Then Harry heard a noise.

It sounded like a giggle.

"Wolfie?" he said.

Polly laughed.

"Polly!" cried Harry. "You rat!"

"Did I scare you?" asked Polly.

"No!" said Harry.

"Well," said Polly,

"it's very dark out here.

Let's go back to the house."